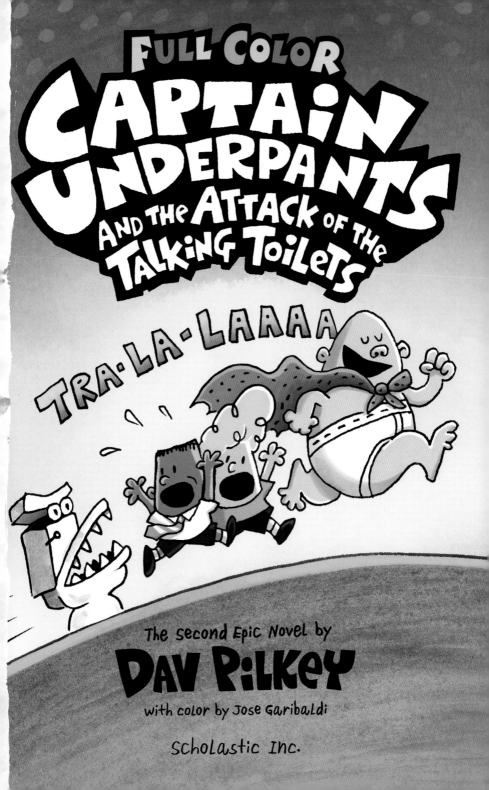

Library of Congress Control Number: 2022938932
ISBN 978-1-338-86430-4

10 9 8 7 6 5 4 3 2   23 24 25 26 27

Cover design by Dav Pilkey and Phil Falco
Book design by Dav Pilkey, Kathleen Westray, and Phil Falco
Color by Jose Garibaldi

Printed in China   62
This edition first printing, March 2023

This book has been approved by

P.E.T.T.
People for
the Ethical
Treatment of
Toilets

To learn more, please visit
planetpilkey.com.

For Alan Boyko

CHAPTERS

FOREWORD:
The Top-Secret Truth About Captain Underpants   7

1. George and Harold   11
2. *This* Story   15
3. The Flashback   19
4. The Invention   25
5. Bigger and Better Things   31
6. The Invention Convention   33
7. Busted   39
8. The Invention Convention Detention   41
9. Captain Underpants and the Attack of the Talking Toilets   45
10. A Big Mistake   53
11. The Invention Convention Detention Suspension   59
12. Things Get Worse   61
13. It's Too Late!   67
14. The Talking Toilet Takeover   71
15. Creamed Chipped Beef to the Rescue!   75

16. The Turbo Toilet 2000   83

17. The Incredibly Graphic Violence Chapter,
    Part 1 (in Flip-O-Rama™)   87

18. Harold and the Purple Ballpoint Pen   103

19. The Incredible Robo-Plunger   107

20. The Incredibly Graphic Violence Chapter,
    Part 2 (in Flip-O-Rama™)   109

21. The Aftermath   123

22. To Make a Long Story Short   127

23. After the Aftermath   128

24. Principals for the Day (or, The Invention
    Convention Detention Suspension Prevention)   129

    Bonus Comic: Dog Man in the Tongue
    of Justice   138

    Fun Facts   155

CHAPTER 1
GEORGE AND HAROLD

This is George Beard and Harold Hutchins. George is the kid on the left with the tie and the flat-top. Harold is the one on the right with the T-shirt and the bad haircut. Remember that now.

Joe's FURNITURE

COME IN AND SEE OUR PRETTY ARMCHAIRS

Depending on who you asked, you'd probably hear a lot of different things about George and Harold.

Their teacher, Ms. Ribble, might say that George and Harold were *disruptive* and *behaviorally challenged*.

Their gym teacher, Mr. Meaner, might add that they were in serious need of a major *attitude adjustment*.

Their principal, Mr. Krupp, would probably have a few more choice words to include, like *sneaky* and *criminally mischievous* and *"I'll get those boys if it's the last thing I . . ."* Well, you get the idea.

But if you asked their parents, they'd probably tell you that George and Harold were smart and sweet and very good-hearted . . . even if they were a bit silly at times.

I'd have to agree with their parents.

But even so, their silliness *did* get them into a lot of trouble, sometimes. In fact, it once got them into so much trouble, they accidentally almost destroyed the whole planet with an army of evil, vicious talking toilets!

But before I can tell you that story, I have to tell you *this* story . . .

CHAPTER 2
THIS STORY

One fine morning at Jerome Horwitz
Elementary School, George and Harold
had just gotten out of their fourth-grade
remedial gym class when they saw a big
sign in the hallway.

It was an announcement for the
Second Annual Invention Convention.

George and Harold had fond memories of last year's Invention Convention, but this year's convention was a bit different. The first-prize winner got to be Principal for the Day.

"Wow," said George. "Whoever gets to be principal gets to make up all the rules for the whole day, and everybody in school has to follow those rules!"

"We have *got* to win first prize this year!" exclaimed Harold.

Just then, George and Harold's principal, Mr. Krupp, showed up.

"A-HA!" he shouted. "I'll bet you two are up to no good!"

"Not really," said George. "We were just reading about this year's contest."

"Yeah," said Harold. "We're going to win first prize in the contest and be *Principals for the Day*!"

"Ha, ha, ha, ha, ha!" laughed Mr. Krupp.
"Do you *honestly* think I'd let you two
enter this year's contest after that stunt
you pulled at *last* year's Invention
Convention?!!?"

George and Harold smiled and thought
back to the First Annual Invention
Convention . . .

CHAPTER 3
THE FLASHBACK

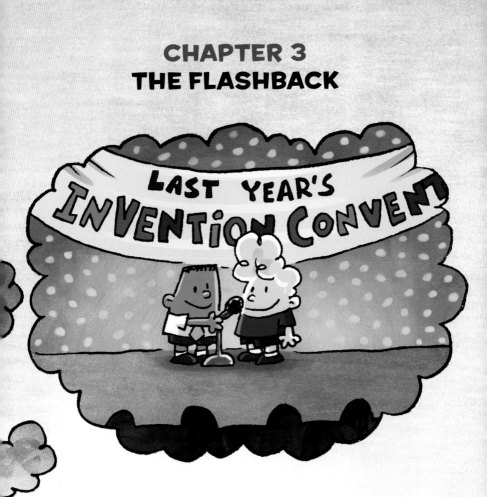

It was about one year earlier, and all of the faculty and students of Jerome Horwitz Elementary School had gathered in the gymnasium for what would later be known as the "Sticky Chair Incident." George and Harold stepped up to the microphone.

"Ladies and gentlemen," said George, "Harold and I have invented something that is guaranteed to keep you all *glued to your seats*!"

"Yes," said Harold. "We call it *glue*."

Mr. Krupp became very angry. "You two did not invent *glue*!" he shouted. He stood up to take the microphone away from Harold, and his chair stood up with him. Everyone in the gymnasium laughed.

The school secretary, Miss Anthrope, stood up to help remove Mr. Krupp's chair from his pants. Her chair stood up with her, too. Everyone in the gymnasium laughed harder.

The other teachers stood up, and—
you guessed it—they were stuck to their
chairs as well. Everyone in the audience
howled with laughter.

One kid stood up to go to the bathroom,
and his chair came up with him, also.
The audience stopped laughing so hard.
They all quickly checked their chairs, and
suddenly, the laughter stopped completely.
Everyone in the whole school was glued to
their seats.

You see, while it was true that George and Harold had not invented glue, they *had* invented a new *kind* of glue. By simply mixing rubber cement with concentrated orange juice mix, they had created a quick-drying, body-heat-activated glue. Then they applied this special glue to every seat in the gymnasium (except theirs) early that morning.

Everybody in the gymnasium was glaring at George and Harold and *seething* with anger.

"I've got a good idea," said George.

"What?" asked Harold.

"RUN!" cried George.

George and Harold were grinning
from ear to ear, remembering their silly
invention and the chaos that followed.

"That was hilarious," laughed Harold.

"Yeah," chuckled George. "It'll be hard
to top that *this* year!"

"Well, you won't get a chance this year,"
said Mr. Krupp. He took out a magnifying
glass and held it up to the fine print on
the sign.

"This contest is open to all students
in the third and fourth grades EXCEPT
George Beard and Harold Hutchins."

"You mean, we can't enter the contest?" asked Harold.

"It's worse than that," laughed Mr. Krupp. "You boys can't even *attend* this year's convention. I'm putting you two in study hall that whole day!" Mr. Krupp turned and walked away, laughing victoriously.

"Rats!" said Harold. "What are we going to do now?"

"Well," said George, "you know the old saying: If you can't join 'em, *beat 'em!*"

CHAPTER 4
THE INVENTION

Early that evening, George and Harold
sneaked back to school with their supplies.
They crept into the gymnasium and
peeked around.

"I think somebody's still in here,"
whispered Harold.

"Oh, it's just Melvin Sneedly," said
George.

Melvin was the school brainiac. He was
busy putting some last-minute touches
on his new invention for the contest.

"We should wait here until he leaves," whispered Harold.

"No way," said George. "He could be here all night! Let's just go over and talk to him."

When Melvin saw George and Harold approaching, he was not happy. "Oh, *no*!" he said. "I'll bet you guys are here to mess with everybody's inventions."

"Nice guess," said George. "Listen, we promise not to mess with *your* invention, if you promise not to tell anybody that you saw *us* here tonight."

Melvin looked lovingly at his invention, and reluctantly agreed. "I promise," he said.

"Great," said George. "Say, what is that invention of yours, anyway? It just looks like a photocopy machine."

"Well, it *used* to be a photocopy machine," said Melvin, "but I've made some major adjustments to it. Now it is an invention that will revolutionize the world. I call it the PATSY 2000."

"It'll revolutionize the world, and you named it *PATSY*???" asked Harold.

"Yes," said Melvin. "PATSY is an acronym for Photo-Atomic Trans-Somgobulating Yectofantriplutonic-zanziptomiser."

"I'm sorry I asked," said Harold.

"Allow me to demonstrate," said Melvin. "The PATSY 2000 can take any two-dimensional image and create a living, breathing, three-dimensional copy of that image. For example, take this ordinary photograph of a mouse."

Melvin placed the photo of the mouse onto the glass screen of the PATSY 2000 and pressed "Start."

The lights in the gymnasium dimmed as all the power in the entire school seemed to get sucked into the PATSY 2000. Soon the machine began to vibrate and hum loudly, and tiny bolts of static electricity snapped out from underneath.

"I hope that thing doesn't explode,"
said Harold.

"Oh, this is *nothing*," said Melvin. "You
should have seen how the PATSY 2000
reacted when I copied a *poodle*!"

Finally, after a series of flashes and loud
zaps, everything stopped. A small *ding*
was heard, then a tiny mouse crawled out
the side door of the PATSY 2000 and onto
the floor.

"Isn't it wonderful?!!?" exclaimed Melvin.

George inspected the mouse closely.

"That's a great trick," George laughed.
"You really had me goin' for a while!"

"It's *not* a trick," cried Melvin. "The
PATSY 2000 really *does* bring photos to
life! I've even created living creatures
from *paintings* and *drawings*!"

"Yeah, *right*!" laughed Harold. "And I
thought *we* were con artists!"

George and Harold walked away
chuckling. It was time to move on to
bigger and better things.

CHAPTER 5
BIGGER AND
BETTER THINGS

George and Harold went to the other end
of the gymnasium, opened their backpacks,
and began to work.

George busied himself by turning all
the spray nozzles on the Automatic Dog-
Washer around, while Harold filled up the
soap tank with India ink.

Then they moved on to the Volcano
Detector. "Will you please pass me the
big bag of butterscotch pudding and a
Phillips-head screwdriver?" asked Harold.

"Sure," said George, as he carefully
inserted eggs into the Ping-Pong
Serve-O-Matic.

CHAPTER 6

THE INVENTION CONVENTION

The following day started out sunny and cheerful. The students and faculty filed into the gymnasium and checked the seats *very* carefully before sitting down.

"Greetings," said Mr. Krupp, who was standing up at the microphone. "You don't need to worry about sticky seats today," he said. "I've taken measures to ensure that *this* Invention Convention won't be a disaster like *last* year's."

MATIC
-WASHER

Everyone settled in as Madison
Mancini, a third grader, stepped onstage to
demonstrate her Automatic Dog-Washer.

"First," said Madison, "you put your dog
in the tub. Then you press this button."

Madison pressed the "Start" button. At
first, nothing happened. Then suddenly,
a spurt of inky black water sprayed up

and out over the crowd. Everyone (except the dog) got soaked, as Madison tried desperately to turn off the sprayers.

"I can't stop it!" she cried. "Someone turned all the nozzles around!"

"Now, *who* could've done that?" asked Mr. Krupp.

Next up was Donny Shoemyer, with his Ping-Pong Serve-O-Matic. He turned the machine on, and immediately it began hurling extra-large grade-A eggs into the crowd.

Phoop!-Phoop!-Phoop!-Phoop!-Phoop! went the machine.

Splat!-Splat!-Splat!-Splat!-Splat! went the eggs.

"I can't turn the machine off!" cried Donny. "Somebody jammed a paper clip into the controller!"

"Now, *who* could've done that?" asked Ms. Ribble.

Freddie Moore's Volcano Detector was also a big flop. When Freddie connected the circuits to the nine-volt battery, a large spring (which had been crammed into the center of his miniature volcano) launched a giant plastic bag of butterscotch pudding high into the crowd.

It landed somewhere between the third and fourth rows. *Splat!*

"Hey!" whined Freddie. "Somebody put pudding in my volcano!"

"Now, *who* could've done that?" asked Mr. Meaner.

The rest of the day went on much the same way, with people shouting everything from "Hey! Who put oatmeal in my solar-powered leaf blower?" to "Hey, who let all the mice out of my treadmill dune buggy?"

It wasn't long before everyone fled the gymnasium, and the Second Annual Invention Convention had to be called off.

"*How could this have happened?!!?*" cried Mr. Krupp as he wiped chocolate syrup, pencil shavings, and cream-of-mushroom soup off his face and shirt. "George and Harold have been in study hall all day long! I put them there *myself*!"

"Um, excuse me, Mr. Krupp," said Melvin Sneedly. "I think I have an answer to your question."

CHAPTER 7
BUSTED

CRASH! went the door to the study hall room. Mr. Krupp stomped in like a crazy person. George and Harold had *never* seen him this upset before.

"You boys are in *SO* MUCH TROUBLE!" Mr. Krupp shouted. "I'm putting you two on PERMANENT DETENTION for the REST OF THE SCHOOL YEAR!"

"Wait a second," cried George. "You can't prove anything!"

"Yeah," said Harold. "We've been here all day!"

Mr. Krupp smiled devilishly, and looked toward the door. "Oh, *Melvin*," he called.

Melvin Sneedly stepped into the room, covered in mustard, eggshells, and shredded coconut.

"They did it," Melvin said, pointing at George and Harold. "I saw 'em last night in the gym!"

"Melvin!" cried George, horrified. "You *promised*!"

"I changed my mind," Melvin said, grinning smugly. "Have fun in detention!"

CHAPTER 8
THE INVENTION CONVENTION DETENTION

After school, Mr. Krupp ushered George and Harold into the detention room and wrote a long sentence on the chalkboard.

"From now on," growled Mr. Krupp, "you boys will spend *two hours a day* after school copying this sentence over and over. I want every chalkboard in this room filled *completely*!"

On his way out the door, Mr. Krupp turned and said with an evil grin, "And if either of you leaves this room for *any* reason, I'm going to *suspend* you both!"

Now, as you might have guessed, writing sentences was nothing new to George and Harold. The two boys waited until Mr. Krupp left the room, then they each took four homemade wooden rods out of their backpacks. The rods had holes in them that George and Harold had drilled in George's dad's woodshop.

George screwed the rods together, while Harold inserted a piece of chalk into each hole.

Then they each took a pole and began copying Mr. Krupp's sentence. Every time they wrote one sentence, the wooden poles made twelve!

After about three and a half minutes, every chalkboard in the room was completely filled.

George and Harold sat down and admired their work.

"We've got a lot of time on our hands now," said George. "Got any ideas?"

"Let's make a new comic book!" said Harold.

So the two boys took out some paper and pens and created an all-new adventure about their favorite superhero. It was called *Captain Underpants and the Attack of the Talking Toilets*.

CHAPTER 10
A BIG MISTAKE

George and Harold sat together in the detention room, reading through their newest comic book and beaming proudly.

"We've got to go to the office and make copies of this," said George, "so we can sell them on the playground tomorrow."

"We can't," said Harold. "Don't you remember? Mr. Krupp said he'd *suspend* us if he caught us leaving this room!"

"Then we won't let him catch us," said George.

George and Harold sneaked out of the
room quietly and crawled down the hall
to the office.

"Uh-oh," said Harold. "There's a bunch
of teachers in there. We'll never get to use
the copy machine."

"Hmmm," said George. "Are there any
other copy machines in this school?"

"How about the one that Melvin had
in the gym?" asked Harold.

"Oh, yeah," said George.

George and Harold crept over to the gym and found the PATSY 2000.

"I wonder if this machine still makes copies," said Harold. "Melvin *did* say that he had made some adjustments to it."

"Oh, he probably just crammed a mouse in there to fool us," said George. "It's the oldest trick in the book. I'm sure the machine still makes regular copies."

George placed the cover of their new comic book facedown on the glass screen and pressed "Start."

All at once, the lights in the whole school dimmed, and the PATSY 2000 began to shake and clunk around wildly. Giant volts of static electricity zapped out the bottom of the machine as a great whirlwind rose from the top. Loose papers and other small objects in the room were sucked into the wind, and they spun above the machine like a raging cyclone.

"I don't think it's supposed to do this!" shouted George over the horrible noise.

Finally, after a series of flashes and loud zaps, the noise, wind, and sparks stopped altogether. The only sound that could be heard was of something groaning and clawing about inside the bloated, battered frame of the PATSY 2000.

"It sounds like something's *alive* inside there," said Harold.

George snatched the comic book from the top of the machine. "Let's get out of here!" he cried.

Just then, a small *ding* was heard, and a full-sized, shiny white toilet emerged from the side of the PATSY 2000. Its teeth were sharp and jagged, and its angry eyeballs glowed with red, swelling veins. "YUM, YUM, EAT 'EM UP!" cried the evil toilet.

Almost immediately, another talking toilet emerged, followed by another and another and *another*. "YUM, YUM, EAT 'EM UP!" they cried.

"Oh, *NO*! Melvin was *RIGHT*!!! The Photo-Atomic Trans-Somgobulating Yectofantriplutoniczanziptomiser really *DOES* create living, breathing, three-dimensional copies of two-dimensional images!" Harold cried convolutedly.

"I've got an idea," said George.

"What?" asked Harold.

"RUN!" cried George.

58

CHAPTER 11
THE INVENTION
CONVENTION DETENTION
SUSPENSION

George and Harold screamed and ran
out the gym door, closing it tightly
behind them.

"A-*HA*!!!" yelled Mr. Krupp, who was
just coming down the hall. "You boys left
the detention room! You know what that
means, don't you?!!?"

"*It wasn't our fault!*" cried Harold.

"*Too* bad!" Mr. Krupp shouted with
delight. "You boys are officially
SUSPENDED!!!"

GYM

"Wait," cried George. "You've got to listen! Behind this door is an army of evil, vicious talk—"

"I don't have to listen to you boys *ever again*," laughed Mr. Krupp. "Now get your stuff and get out of this school!"

"But. . . but. . . ." Harold stammered, "you don't understa—"

"GET OUT!!!" Mr. Krupp screamed.

George and Harold groaned and walked to their lockers to collect their stuff.

"Gosh," said Harold. "In one day we've gotten a detention, a suspension, *and* we've created an army of evil talking toilets who want to take over the world."

"That's a pretty bad day, even by *our* standards," said George.

"Oh, well," said Harold. "I just hope things don't get any worse."

CHAPTER 12
THINGS GET WORSE

Word spread quickly throughout the office that George and Harold had been suspended. The teachers rushed out to cheer and laugh at the two boys.

"You're in big trouble now," chuckled Miss Anthrope. "I can't wait to call your parents and tell them the news!"

"Let's take their desks outside and chop them up!" cried Ms. Ribble.

"Let's throw a party in the gym!" shouted Mr. Meaner.

"*NOOO!*" cried George. "Whatever you do, *DON'T* open the door to the gym!"

"We can do whatever we like," snarled Mr. Meaner as he dashed over to the gymnasium door. "Look, I'm opening the door!" He quickly opened the gym door. "Now I'm closing the door," he said.

"Now I'm opening the door again, and now I'm—AAAAAAAAHH mmblemble gluh!"

An evil toilet had stuck its mouth through the door, snapped Mr. Meaner up, and swallowed him whole! *Flusssssh!*

The Talking Toilets then pushed their way through the open gymnasium doors and spilled out into the hallway.

"YUM, YUM, EAT 'EM UP!" the toilets bellowed. "YUM, YUM, EAT 'EM UP!"

The teachers couldn't believe their eyes. They screamed and ran for their lives. Only Mr. Krupp, Ms. Ribble, and George and Harold remained, frozen in fear. They watched, paralyzed, as the Talking Toilets came nearer and nearer. Finally, Ms. Ribble pointed at the toilets and snapped her fingers.

SNAP!

"Go away," she cried. "Go away this minute!" But the toilets didn't listen. They moved closer and closer.

64

Finally, Ms. Ribble turned and ran. Mr. Krupp, however, just stood there in a daze. George and Harold looked up at him.

"Uh-oh," said Harold. "Did she just *snap her fingers*?!!?"

"Yep," said George. "Now we're *really* in trouble."

And George was right, for at that moment, Mr. Krupp had begun to change. A silly, heroic smile came over his face as he stood defiantly before his foes.

"I'll put a stop to you vile villains," he said fearlessly. "But first, I need some *supplies*!!!"

Mr. Krupp turned and dashed to his office. George and Harold ran after him.

"Why did Ms. Ribble have to snap her fingers?!!?" cried Harold. *"Why?!!?"*

"Never mind that," cried George. "Mr. Krupp is turning into Captain Underpants! We've got to pour water over his head before it's too late!"

CHAPTER 13
IT'S TOO LATE!

When George and Harold reached Mr. Krupp's office, they found only his clothes, shoes, and toupee on the floor.

"Look," said Harold. "The window is open, and one of the red curtains is missing."

"What do we do now?" asked George. "Do we save Captain Underpants, or do we stay here and get eaten by a bunch of toilets?"

"Hmmm . . . Let me think about that one!" said Harold as he climbed out the window.

George quickly collected Mr. Krupp's
things and shoved them into his backpack.
Then he jumped out the window after
Harold. The two boys slid down the flagpole
and ran off after Captain Underpants.

"Where does he think he's going?"
asked George.

"I have *no* idea," said Harold. "But
we'd better run fast because I think we're
being *followed*!"

Captain Underpants dashed through the backyards of some nearby houses and collected pairs of underwear from the clotheslines.

"Mommy," said a little boy looking out his window, "a man in a red cape just stole our underwear."

"And now two boys are being chased by a ferocious-looking toilet with sharp, pointy teeth, screaming, 'Yum, yum, eat 'em up!'"

"Yeah, *right*!" laughed his mother. "Just how *gullible* do you think I am?!!?"

70

CHAPTER 14
THE TALKING TOILET
TAKEOVER

When Captain Underpants was finished commandeering the underwear of local civilians, he dashed back to Jerome Horwitz Elementary to save the day.

The school was now overrun with chaos. Ms. Ribble came tearing out the door, followed by several evil toilets.

"Help me!" she cried. "They've swallowed every teacher in the whole building except me!"

"Don't worry, ma'am, I won't let them eat you up," Captain Underpants said, as a toilet ate her up.

"Oops!" said Captain Underpants.

Now only George, Harold, and Captain Underpants were left. They stood on the front lawn of the school, completely surrounded by hungry, drooling toilets.

"YUM, YUM, EAT 'EM UP!" the Talking Toilets chanted. "YUM, YUM, EAT 'EM UP! YUM, YUM, EAT 'EM UP! YUM, YUM, EAT 'EM UP!"

"We're *doomed*!" cried Harold.

"*Never* underestimate the power of underwear!" cried Captain Underpants, as he stretched and shot underwear into the waiting mouths of the Talking Toilets.

Unfortunately, the toilets just swallowed the underwear whole. It only seemed to make them hungrier and hungrier.

"If only we could think of something that would make them really *sick*," said George.

"Yeah," Harold continued, "something so vile and disgusting, it would make them all *blow their cookies* and writhe in agony!"

Suddenly, George and Harold's faces lit up. "CAFETERIA FOOD!" they shouted. And faster than a speeding waistband, our three heroes dashed into the school.

CHAPTER 15
CREAMED CHIPPED BEEF TO THE RESCUE!

George, Harold, and Captain Underpants got inside the school safely and closed the front door behind them. "I think the toilets are all outside," said George.

"But not for long," said Harold.

Quickly they ran to the school's kitchen and discovered a cart holding a large vat of something green and sludgy.

"Yuck," said George, holding his nose. "What *is* that stuff?"

"I think it's tomorrow's lunch," said Harold.

"Perfect!" said George. "I never thought I'd be *glad* to see creamed chipped beef!"

Together, they wheeled the tub of stinky green glop down the hallway and out the side door of the school. Captain Underpants sat on the cart and stretched a pair of underwear over his head like a slingshot.

George stood over him, scooped some cafeteria food into the underwear, and stretched it back. Harold wheeled the cart toward the Talking Toilets.

"Tra-La-Laaaaa!!!!" shouted Captain Underpants loudly.

The Talking Toilets turned and saw our three heroes. All at once, they shouted "YUM, YUM, EAT 'EM UP!" and the chase was on!

Harold pulled the cart across the playground as the toilets zipped after them.

"Fire One!" cried Captain Underpants.

George shot a glob of creamed chipped beef into the first toilet's mouth. The toilet swallowed it whole.

Harold kept pulling, as George scooped another serving into the underwear and pulled it back.

"Fire Two!" cried Captain Underpants.

Zip! went the cafeteria food, right into the *second* toilet's mouth.

The whole process repeated itself until every last toilet had swallowed at least two servings of creamed chipped beef.

"We're almost out of ammo!" Captain Underpants shouted.

"And I don't think I can run anymore," said Harold, huffing and puffing.

"Don't worry. . . *look*!" said George, pointing at the toilets.

They had all slowed down and were beginning to groan and wobble around. Their eyes crossed, and they turned an odd shade of green.

"Look out," cried Harold. "I think they're gonna *hurl*!"

And that's just what they did!
George, Harold, and Captain
Underpants watched as the toilets
upchucked everything they had eaten
during the day. The creamed chipped
beef, the underwear, even the teachers
all came out without a scratch.

Then the toilets spun around in small circles and fell to the ground, dead.

George checked the teachers. "They're *alive*," he said. "*Unconscious*, but alive!"

"Wow," said Harold. "That was *easy*!"

"*Too* easy," said George.

"What do you mean?" asked Harold.

George pulled their comic book out of his backpack and showed it to Harold. "Remember how the PATSY 2000 turned everything on the front cover of our comic book to life?" he asked.

"Yeah, so?" said Harold.

"Well," said George, as he pointed to the Turbo Toilet 2000 on the front cover of the comic. "We haven't seen *him* yet!"

CHAPTER 16
THE TURBO TOILET 2000

Suddenly, the Turbo Toilet 2000 came charging out the front door of the school with a terrible *CRASH*! The earth rumbled beneath its mighty footsteps as nearly a ton of twisting steel and raging porcelain descended upon our heroes.

"You three meddling fools *may* have destroyed my army of Talking Toilets," screamed the Turbo Toilet 2000, "but you're *all out* of cafeteria food! How are you gonna stop *ME*?!!?"

"I'll tell you how," Captain Underpants said boldly. "With *Wedgie Power!*"

"*Wait*, Captain Underpants!" cried George. "You can't fight that thing! He'll rip you to pieces!"

"Boys," said Captain Underpants nobly, "I *must* fight valiantly for Truth, Justice, and *all* that is Pre-Shrunk and Cottony!"

Captain Underpants leaped onto the
Turbo Toilet 2000, and the battle began.
    "I sure hope this doesn't lead to
incredibly graphic violence," said Harold.
    "Me, too," said George.

CHAPTER 17
THE INCREDIBLY GRAPHIC VIOLENCE CHAPTER, PART 1 (IN FLIP-O-RAMA™)

WARNING:

The following chapter contains intense scenes showing a man in his underwear battling a giant toilet. Please do not try this at home.

PILKEY® BRAND
ᗷ-RAMA

HERE'S HOW IT WORKS!

STEP 1
First, place your *left* hand inside the dotted lines marked "LEFT HAND HERE." Hold the book open *flat*.

STEP 2
Grasp the *right-hand* page with your right thumb and index finger (inside the dotted lines marked "RIGHT THUMB HERE").

STEP 3
Now *quickly* flip the right-hand page back and forth until the picture appears to be *animated*.

(For extra fun, try adding your own sound-effects!)

FLIP-O-RAMA 1

(pages 91 and 93)

Remember, flip *only* page 91.
While you are flipping, be sure you
can see the picture on page 91
and the one on page 93.
If you flip quickly, the two
pictures will start to look like
<u>one</u> *animated* picture.

Don't forget to
add your own sound-effects!

LEFT HAND HERE

WEDGIE POWER
VS.
POTTY POWER

RIGHT
THUMB
HERE

RIGHT
INDEX
FINGER
HERE

92

WEDGIE POWER
VS.
POTTY POWER

FLIP-O-RAMA 2

(pages 95 and 97)

Remember, flip *only* page 95.
While you are flipping, be sure you
can see the picture on page 95
and the one on page 97.
If you flip quickly, the two
pictures will start to look like
<u>one</u> *animated* picture.

Don't forget to
add your own sound-effects!

LEFT HAND HERE

OH, *NO!!!*
THE POTTY POWER
PUNCH PREVAILS!

RIGHT
THUMB
HERE

RIGHT
INDEX
FINGER
HERE

96

OH, *NO!!!*
THE POTTY POWER
PUNCH PREVAILS!

FLIP-O-RAMA 3

(pages 99 and 101)

Remember, flip *only* page 99.
While you are flipping, be sure you
can see the picture on page 99
and the one on page 101.
If you flip quickly, the two
pictures will start to look like
<u>one</u> *animated* picture.

Don't forget to
add your own sound-effects!

LEFT HAND HERE

THE CARNIVOROUS
COMMODE CAPTURES
THE CAPTAIN!

RIGHT
THUMB
HERE

THE CARNIVOROUS COMMODE CAPTURES THE CAPTAIN!

CHAPTER 18
HAROLD AND THE PURPLE BALLPOINT PEN

Everything seemed hopeless. Captain Underpants had slipped and fallen into the mouth of the Turbo Toilet 2000, and now the giant toilet was coming after George and Harold!

"Ha, ha, ha, ha, ha!" laughed the powerful porcelain predator. "Once I have eaten you two kids up, I will *take over the world*!"

"Not if *we* have anything to say about it!" yelled George.

George and Harold ran into the school and locked the door behind them. The Turbo Toilet 2000 banged against the door with its fists, shouting, "You boys can't hide in there forever!"

George and Harold ran to the gym.

"I've got a plan," said George. "We need to invent a character who can defeat a giant robot toilet."

"How about a giant robot urinal?" asked Harold. "We can call it *The Urinator*!"

"No way!" said George. "They'll never let us get away with that in a children's book. We're skating on *thin ice* as it is!"

"All right," said Harold, "how about a giant plunger robot? He can carry a really big plunger, and—"

"*That's it!*" cried George.

So Harold took out his purple ballpoint pen and began to draw.

"Give him *laser* eyes," said George.

"All right," said Harold.

"And give him turbo-atomic rocket boosters," said George.

"Got it," said Harold.

"And make him obey our every command," said George.

"I'm *way* ahead of you," said Harold.

Harold finished his drawing, and
George inspected it carefully.

"This just *might* work," said George.

"Yeah," said Harold, "if the PATSY 2000
can hold out."

The boys turned and looked at the dented,
cracked, and beaten-up machine laying
on its side in the corner. George and
Harold pushed the PATSY 2000 upright
and dusted it off.

"Come on, PATSY, old girl," said
George. "We really need you now!"

"Yeah," said Harold. "The fate of the
entire planet is in our hands!"

CHAPTER 19
THE INCREDIBLE ROBO-PLUNGER

George took Harold's picture and placed it on the screen of the PATSY 2000 and pressed "Start."

The lights around them dimmed as the weary machine began to shake and smoke. Lightning bolts zapped, thunder clapped, and the whole gymnasium shook with Photo-Atomic Trans-Somgobulatory Yectofantriplutoniczanziptic energy.

"C'mon, PATSY!" George shouted over the horrible noise. "You can do it, baby!"

Finally a small *ding* was heard, and the
PATSY 2000 coughed up a huge, metallic
behemoth. It rose up and stood valiantly
before George and Harold. It was the
Incredible Robo-Plunger.

"*Hooray!*" cried George. "It *worked*!"

"Way to go, PATSY!" Harold cheered.
"Now let's get outside and kick some
Turbo Toilet Tushy!"

WARNING:

The following chapter contains terribly naughty scenes depicting a giant toilet getting its shiny hiney kicked.

All toilet violence was carefully monitored by P.E.T.T. (People for the Ethical Treatment of Toilets).

No actual toilets were harmed during the making of this chapter.

FLIP-O-RAMA 4

(pages 111 and 113)

Remember, flip *only* page 111.
While you are flipping, be sure you
can see the picture on page 111
and the one on page 113.
If you flip quickly, the two
pictures will start to look like
<u>one</u> *animated* picture.

Don't forget to
add your own sound-effects!

LEFT HAND HERE

THE INCREDIBLE ROBO-PLUNGER TO THE RESCUE!

RIGHT
THUMB
HERE

112

THE INCREDIBLE
ROBO-PLUNGER TO
THE RESCUE!

FLIP-O-RAMA 5

(pages 115 and 117)

Remember, flip *only* page 115.
While you are flipping, be sure you
can see the picture on page 115
and the one on page 117.
If you flip quickly, the two
pictures will start to look like
<u>one</u> *animated* picture.

Don't forget to
add your own sound-effects!

LEFT HAND HERE

THE INCREDIBLE ROBO-PLUNGER KICKS THE TT 2000'S TUSHY!

RIGHT
THUMB
HERE

RIGHT
INDEX
FINGER
HERE

THE INCREDIBLE ROBO-PLUNGER KICKS THE TT 2000'S TUSHY!

FLIP-O-RAMA 6

(pages 119 and 121)

Remember, flip *only* page 119.
While you are flipping, be sure you
can see the picture on page 119
and the one on page 121.
If you flip quickly, the two
pictures will start to look like
<u>one</u> *animated* picture.

Don't forget to
add your own sound-effects!

LEFT HAND HERE

THE TT 2000
TAKES THE
PLUNGE!

RIGHT
THUMB
HERE

RIGHT
INDEX
FINGER
HERE

120

THE TT 2000 TAKES THE PLUNGE!

CHAPTER 21
THE AFTERMATH

The Incredible Robo-Plunger had defeated the evil Turbo Toilet 2000, but George and Harold's problems weren't over yet. They reached into the crumpled mouth of the TT 2000 and pulled out their principal.

"What happened here?" cried Mr. Krupp. "The school has been *destroyed*, the teachers are all *unconscious*, and I'm standing here in my *underwear*!"

"Uh-oh!" Harold whispered. "Captain
Underpants must have gotten toilet water
on his head. He's turned back into
Principal Krupp!"

George took Mr. Krupp's clothes and
hair out of his backpack and handed them
to him.

"I'm ruined!" Principal Krupp whined
as he dressed himself. "I'm going to be
held responsible for this mess! I'm going
to lose my job!"

"Maybe not," said George. "We can fix everything, and clean up this whole mess."

"Yeah," said Harold, "but it'll cost you!"

"Cost me *what*?" asked Mr. Krupp.

"Well," said George, "we'd like you to cancel our detention *and* our suspension!"

"And we'd also like to be *Principals for the Day*!" said Harold.

"All right," said Mr. Krupp. "If you can really fix *everything*, you've got a deal!"

George and Harold turned and spoke to
the Incredible Robo-Plunger.

"All right, robot guy," said George,
"make yourself useful and pick up all this
mess!"

"Yeah, and fix up the school, too," said
Harold. "Use your laser eyes to repair all
the broken windows and stuff!"

"And when you're done," said George,
"take all the evidence and fly it up to
Uranus."

"And don't come back!" said Harold.

CHAPTER 22
TO MAKE A LONG STORY SHORT

The robot obeyed.

CHAPTER 23
AFTER THE
AFTERMATH

The Incredible Robo-Plunger soared off into space just as the teachers began to regain consciousness.

"I just had the strangest dream," said Ms. Ribble. "It was all about these evil toilets who wanted to take over the world."

"We had the same dream, too," said the other teachers.

"Well," said Mr. Krupp, "things turned out all right after all!"

"Not quite," said George. "It's *payback* time!"

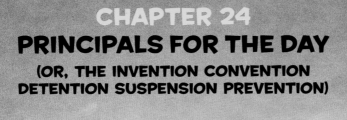

CHAPTER 24
PRINCIPALS FOR THE DAY
(OR, THE INVENTION CONVENTION DETENTION SUSPENSION PREVENTION)

"Attention, students," said George over the intercom the following day. "This is Principal George. You are all excused from classes today. There will be no homework or tests, and everybody gets an A+ for the day."

"That's right," said Principal Harold. "Also, we are hosting an all-day recess outside, complete with free pizza, french fries, cotton candy, and a live DJ. Now go outside and play."

129

Principal George and Principal Harold strolled out to the playground to behold their glorious domain. George got a slice of pepperoni pizza, while Harold made himself a banana split at the all-you-can-eat ice-cream sundae bar.

"It's *good* to be the principal!" said George.

"Yep," said Harold. "I wish we could be principals every day!"

Later, George and Harold paid a visit to the unfortunate folks who were spending the day writing sentences in the detention room. All the teachers were there, along with Mr. Krupp and Melvin Sneedly.

Mr. Krupp looked out the window at the all-day recess celebration going on outside.

"How are you boys going to *pay* for all that ice cream and pizza?" he asked.

"Oh, we sold some stuff," said Harold.

"What did you sell?" asked Mr. Krupp.

"Your antique walnut desk and leather chair," said George. "And all the furniture in the teachers' lounge."

"WHAT?!!?" screamed Mr. Krupp.

"Umm . . . I think we'd better leave now," said Harold.

I will be very, very, very very, very, very, very, very nice to "George the Great", and "The Amazing Harold". I will be very, very, very, very very, very, ve

George and Harold left the detention
room in a hurry. Miss Anthrope snapped
her fingers at them.

SNAP!

"Come back here right now!" she
yelled.

"Uh-oh," said George. "Did Miss
Anthrope just *snap her fingers?*"

134

Within seconds, Mr. Krupp dashed out of the detention room and ran down the hallway toward his office. He had a goofy, heroic, *all-too-familiar-looking* smile on his face.

"Oh, no!" cried Harold.
"Here we go *again*!" said George.

3

4

16

FUN FACT #1

When he was in the third grade, Dav Pilkey made a comic book called *Captain Underpants and the Attack of the Talking Toilet*. It was about an evil scientist who created a potion that brought things to life. The scientist flushed the dangerous potion down a toilet, hoping to get rid of it. Unfortunately, it brought the toilet to life instead. That simple comic book story created in 1975 was the inspiration for this epic novel.

FUN FACT #2

You might notice a theme in George and Harold's comic books: The gym teacher always gets attacked by the villains, but nobody seems to care. This theme occurs again and again because many* of Dav Pilkey's former gym teachers were REALLY, REALLY MEAN to him. So let this be a lesson to gym teachers all over the world: Be nice to your students, or some day they might grow up and get revenge by making fun of you in their epic novels!

*Note: Dav's lawyer told him to use the word *many*.

FUN FACT #3

The term *Invention Convention* was coined by Dav's Uncle Peter. Peter Pilkey** is a retired schoolteacher from Berea, Ohio, who used to host an Invention Convention at his school every year.

**Note: Despite popular speculation, Dav's Uncle Peter has never had anything to do with a peck of pickled peppers.

FUN FACT #4

The little girl who appears on page 34 is Dav Pilkey's niece, Madison. She was two years old when this book was first released.

FUN FACT #5

George and Harold are both based on Dav Pilkey when he was a kid. Like George and Harold, Dav Pilkey was the class clown. He made comics, got in lots of trouble with his teachers and principal, and even switched the letters around on signs and bulletin boards.

FUN FACT #6

Melvin Sneedly was based on a real person who was in Dav Pilkey's class. He used to finish his work before everyone else, then grade his own papers and give himself an A+. He was a big tattletale, too.

ABOUT THE
AUTHOR-ILLUSTRATOR

When Dav Pilkey was a kid, he was diagnosed with ADHD and dyslexia. Dav was so disruptive in class that his teachers made him sit out in the hallway every day. Luckily, Dav loved to draw and make up stories. He spent his time in the hallway creating his own original comic books — the very first adventures of Dog Man and Captain Underpants.

In college, Dav met a teacher who encouraged him to write and illustrate for kids. He took her advice and created his first book, WORLD WAR WON, which won a national competition in 1986. Dav made many other books before being awarded the California Young Reader Medal for DOG BREATH (1994) and the Caldecott Honor for THE PAPERBOY (1996).

In 2002, Dav published his first full-length graphic novel for kids, called THE ADVENTURES OF SUPER DIAPER BABY. It was both a USA Today and New York Times bestseller. Since then, he has published more than a dozen full-length graphic novels for kids, including the bestselling Dog Man and Cat Kid Comic Club series.

Dav's stories are semi-autobiographical and explore universal themes that celebrate friendship, empathy, and the triumph of the good-hearted.

When he is not making books for kids, Dav loves to kayak with his wife in the Pacific Northwest.

Learn more at Pilkey.com.